Dear Parents:

Congratulations! Your child is taking the first steps on an exciting journey. The destination? Independent reading!

STEP INTO READING® will help your child get there. The program offers five steps to reading success. Each step includes fun stories and colorful art or photographs. In addition to original fiction and books with favorite characters, there are Step into Reading Non-Fiction Readers, Phonics Readers and Boxed Sets, Sticker Readers, and Comic Readers—a complete literacy program with something to interest every child.

Learning to Read, Step by Step!

Ready to Read Preschool–Kindergarten
• big type and easy words • rhyme and rhythm • picture clues
For children who know the alphabet and are eager to begin reading.

Reading with Help Preschool–Grade 1
• basic vocabulary • short sentences • simple stories
For children who recognize familiar words and sound out new words with help.

Reading on Your Own Grades 1–3
• engaging characters • easy-to-follow plots • popular topics
For children who are ready to read on their own.

Reading Paragraphs Grades 2–3
• challenging vocabulary • short paragraphs • exciting stories
For newly independent readers who read simple sentences with confidence.

Ready for Chapters Grades 2–4
• chapters • longer paragraphs • full-color art
For children who want to take the plunge into chapter books but still like colorful pictures.

STEP INTO READING® is designed to give every child a successful reading experience. The grade levels are only guides; children will progress through the steps at their own speed, developing confidence in their reading.

Remember, a lifetime love of reading starts with a single step!

Step into Reading, Random House, and the Random House colophon are registered trademarks of Penguin Random House LLC.

Visit us on the Web!
StepIntoReading.com
rhcbooks.com

Educators and librarians, for a variety of teaching tools, visit us at RHTeachersLibrarians.com

ISBN 978-0-593-12208-2 (trade) — ISBN 978-0-593-12209-9 (lib. bdg.)

Printed in the United States of America

10 9 8 7 6 5 4 3 2 1

nickelodeon

HOORAY FOR FRIENDS!

by Delphine Finnegan

based on the teleplay
"Anyu's Friendship Party" by
James Backshall and Jeff Sweeney

illustrated by Dave Aikins

Random House 🏠 New York

Penny is taking an ice bath.
Her friend Anyu calls her.
Anyu needs Penny's help!

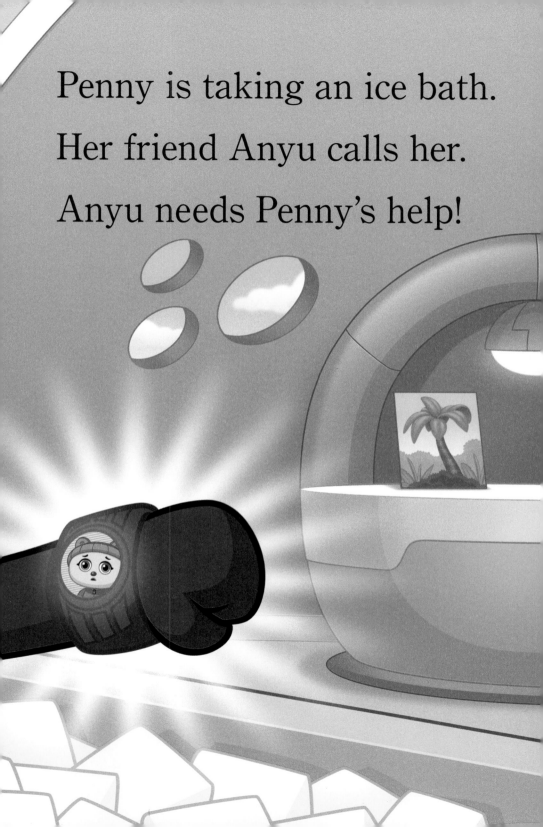

Penny races
to Anyu's island
in her Aqua Wing.

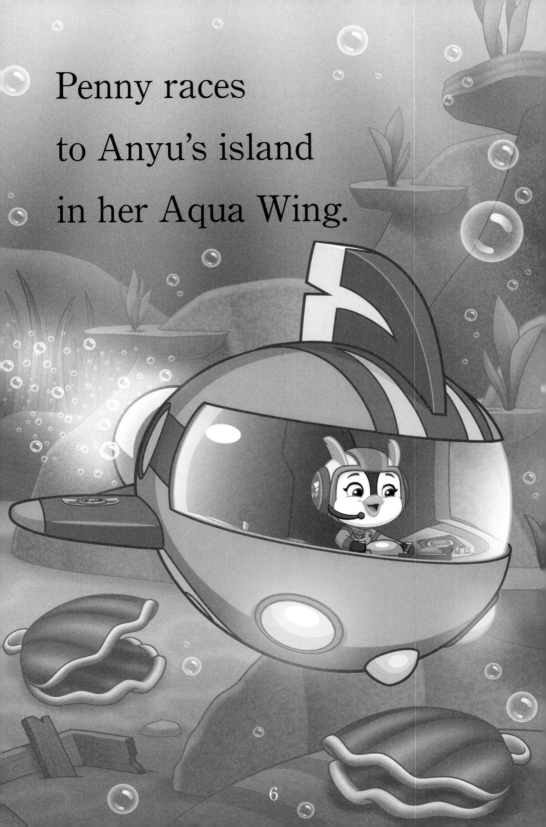

Anyu is having a party.

The party is today!

How can she invite

all her friends in time?

Penny calls Top Wing.
The team will help
deliver Anyu's invitations!

Penny takes the invitations
to Top Wing's headquarters.
Uh-oh.
Salty's invitation
is left behind!

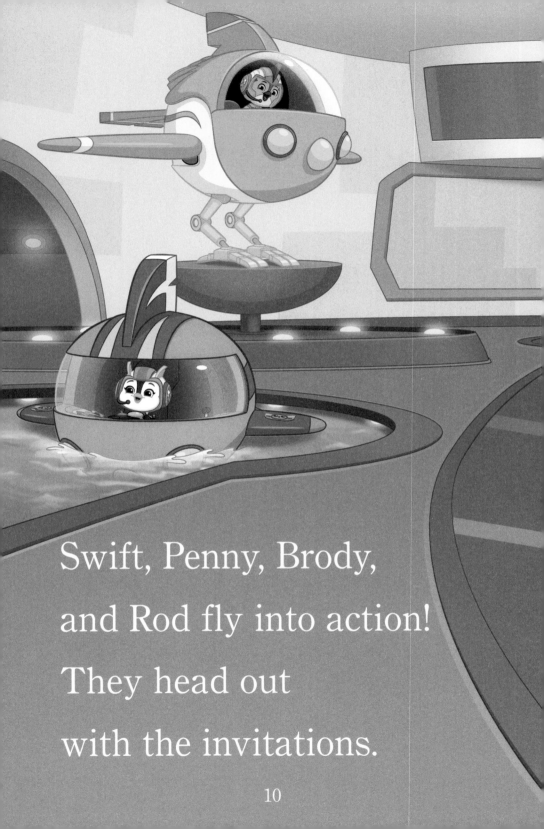

Swift, Penny, Brody,
and Rod fly into action!
They head out
with the invitations.

They will take
Anyu's friends
to the party!

Back on the island,
Anyu finds
Salty's invitation.

She takes the rowboat.

She will get

the invitation to Salty!

Swift picks up Tina
in the Flash Wing.

Brody and Timmy
take the Splash Wing.

Rod is in the Road Wing
with Sammy at his side.

Penny tows
two turtles
to the party!

Anyu tries
to row the boat.

The oars float away.

She is stuck!

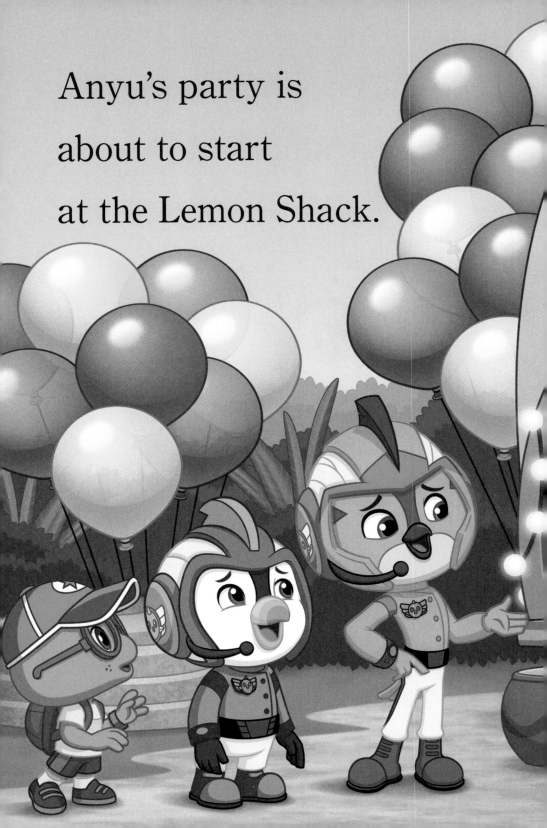

Anyu's party is about to start at the Lemon Shack.

Where is Salty?

Where is Anyu?

Penny races
to the rescue!
Penny saves Anyu!

They find Salty
and invite him.

They all head
to the Lemon Shack.
Everyone is having fun.

Salty brings a cake.

Yum!

What a great party.

Hooray for friends!